CAPITAL QUEER

CAPITAL QUEER:

A PRIDE CELEBRATION FROM
WASHINGTON WRITERS'
PUBLISHING HOUSE

EDITED BY JONA COLSON AND CAROLINE BOCK

Washington Writers' Publishing House
Washington, D.C.

COVER DESIGN by Dave Ring
TYPOGRAPHY by Barbara Shaw

ISBN 978-1-941551-51-6

Library of Congress Control Number: 2025935071

WASHINGTON WRITERS' PUBLISHING HOUSE
2814 5th Street, NE, #1301
Washington, D.C. 20017

To all in the LGBTQ+ community, and to all the allies, friends, and family, who believe in a diverse, inclusive, equitable, and rainbow-filled world, *Capital Queer* is for you.

TABLE OF CONTENTS

US, AT LAST

EMILY HOLLAND

Seven years is a long time, a friend tells us. And
they are right, in some ways. One night in the desert
we talked of marriage until the stars faded. We were so
small, so seemingly insignificant. We slept on different
sides of the bed and for a moment it felt as if everything
had changed. I am always afraid of change, but I love
to party, think I could learn to want the rings, the vows.
There are too many ways to live in I love you.
Back East, trees turn overnight, swap their greens
for yellow and red. Everywhere's a small town
where we only know what we can't say. Look,
someone else's wedding on the Vermont hilltop.
Perfect weather. Can't you see them? Kissing
at the end of the world like nothing else matters.

NOCTURNE

KIM ROBERTS

Not every sound is a wolf;
not every weight a succubus.
          My love snores gently
like a soft ruminant
lingering in our field

under a turning arc of stars.
Her heart's a deep pocket.
          Overnight, her eyelids transform
to willow leaves, her fingers brushing
her cheek become curved branches,

and I shelter in her cool shadow.
The breeze through tossing leaves
          translates slanted light
to the moon, makes a cratered
dapple on the ground, and a fringe

to hide among. But she is braided
by a lack of guile as I stretch out
          against her trunk, and the sound
of her—breathing in, breathing out—
is a ribbon of gentle wind.

Then a creaky door echoes
in the hollow room
             of her intestines. She leans
into my warmth, mutters,
steals the blanket,

her breath tinged with fescue
circling like night's coronation.
             All night,
I rock in the umbra of her branches,
determined to conceal nothing.

UNPACKING ON THE L2

SUNU CHANDY

Entering the L2, a meeting in her headphones
the bus driver stops her. Half paying attention
she thinks it's something about her bus fare, but he keeps
gesturing her towards him and so she stops. He says
to her: *Hope this isn't offensive, but are you gay?* She gives
a complex answer involving phrases
like nonbinary presenting and queer without
checking his box, but he correctly understands
the answer as enough of a version of a yes. And so,
continues his inquiry. He explains it's not that he thinks
gay people shouldn't get married, it's just he thinks
that maybe they shouldn't be parents. And some of his gay colleagues
back at the bus depot got upset at him for saying that.
But, what do you think? You wouldn't be mad if I said that, right?
My spouse, often not hot-headed, paused and responded:
Hmm, where do you think you got that idea? Let's unpack that.
He explained that he thought boys should have
fathers, don't you think? And my tomboy spouse, in her home
with mostly just her mother, grandmother and sister,
came forward with evidence. She said she knew a lot of
young men and other people who were raised just by their mamas
and grew up to be fine. She does know this to be true.
He seemed to pause, and she continued,

to be sure, a father might be a nice to have, but with so many separated
families, that's not always the case, right? And so, they kept chatting.
And then she explained she needed to get back to her meeting,
pointing to her headphones, her colleague having heard this entire
exchange. And it was not until afterwards, as she was passing
by to exit the bus, just across the street from our home
filled with me relearning eighth grade algebra, and our daughter
learning how to make the family whole meals from Hello Fresh,
did she mention this part. *You know, my beautiful wife*
and I might get a lot of things wrong. But I do think we are good
parents to our daughter. She's fourteen. She's in middle
school now. And with that, she went to give that bus driver
a fist bump. And at that moment, at that bus stop, steps from our home,
the bus driver got up from his seat. He unlatched the gate
that kept him in his seat. He came forward, towards her,
he came forward and said: *May I, give you,*
a hug? And when I tell my friends this story,
they ask me if my wife is some kind of prophet. And I beam,
because, I know many of us like to think we have good hearts,
but this one, she must have her mother's wild grace,
in addition to her own, wild patience, too.

THE GRANDDAUGHTER

SAUNDRA ROSE MALEY

Down deep in the miles of mines
of the Allegheny mountains

my grandfather crawled for years
his shoulders cramped by rock—

he had no wings only a pick
and shovel—so he drank

his whiskey and told me once
that he knew if he could get

his shoulders through
he could get his whole body

through—he told me this as if
it were a secret—me—told me

with my secrets—the one who lost
the notebook where I took his story

down that one day he spoke only
to me about those mines—his mines

told me—the granddaughter
who gave him no great grandchildren

because I love women
the way he did—to love a woman—

how can that be bad

NEW RULE

BERNARD WELT

Sonnets suck, cause they just remind us
Spring and flowers and all that junk—nobody
Living can even remember that stuff. So
When you try to talk about love without
Breaking my heart, could you just tell me
About winter and funerals and orphans,
I'll know you're lying anyway but at least
It won't seem utterly ridiculous and seriously,
Kind of offensive, because what I don't want,
What I don't need now, pal, is more of this
Kind of lining me up to buy into some concept
Propping up a social order that you care more
About than my arms, my eyes, my lips, which
Really, are actually more beautiful than ever.

TRAINS DO

HIRAM LAREW

My *I am too* is like a
　　　　first cousin to your *Really* —

Yes
Up and down we agree that
　　　　those who we loved wildly
　　　　we loved for their root soup
　　　　I know that you know
　　　　that's true

And of course it's hard to sort out
　　　　but don't you also think trains go
　　　　　　　　and do what they do
　　　　　　　　just so
　　　　　　　　we can smoke over gossips

Well as I said
　　　　I'll bet the next cup of coffee
　　　　　　　　that my *I am too* is just like
　　　　　　　　home to you
　　　　　　　　and your *Really* —

So, yes, take a bite of my sandwich.

SELF-KNOWLEDGE IS NEGATIVE SPACE

CHARLOTTE VAN SCHAACK

It's not the celebration I care for
so much as the crowd. I want swaddling
as if the infantile queer I am naturally
deserves coddling and a stable childhood.
Progressives like a bassinet make me think
I am well adjusted, three years in the world.
There's nothing special to being
part of DC's five percent, or what seems
to be half my college, or all
my friends. I've never done poppers
or bought a vibrator, but if I did
I am sure it would die on me
or go as untouched. There is not enough
ecstasy to capsize my displacement.
Before I was closeted,
I wondered what kind of people I'd kiss
in college. If I'd lean deeply
with tongue at crowded parties.
I like girls, and I've come to terms
that I like boys, and everyone is beautiful.
I still don't know who to talk to
about all these things.
So many poets have already

laid claim to the sun and moon and stars.
Maybe Jupiter will care to lend
her deep crying storm to catch my words.
I didn't really want a taste of anyone,
just to be known by them in my want
for companionship. My body
must learn against its training and
against again.

A VILLANELLE FOR LOST QUILTBAGGERS

CHRIS BILES

Each day you walk a chasm's edge in fear
with worry rubbing like a grain of sand –
Despair! to wander through this world as queer.

So builds volcanic pressure to adhere,
suppress yourself – and do or don't, you're damned,
coerced to walk that chasm's edge in fear.

Tall cliffs descend to dark unknown frontier.
To stay or go? Uncertainty commands –
Despair! to wander through this world as queer.

But then, *their touch*, and lightning flashes clear,
a fierce illumination of the land.
So as you walk the chasm's edge in fear,

eyes wide, you see the cliffs are not so sheer
and down below are beaches warm and grand.
New breath to wander through this world as queer –

Descend! go barefoot, holding hands, revere
this freedom and just dance as love demands.
No need to stay at chasm's edge with fear –
Descend! then proudly walk this world as queer.

QUEER CLUB

AVA SERRA

Imur the androgynous king turns into the neon-castoff alley with an archway of ebony brick off P St and 15th. You know the area—that block with the comedy club, farm-to-table dinner spot, and abandoned Whole Foods from the era of Amazon's union-busting, human rights-violating supremacy. You know, back then—when cars were still petroleum-drunk, public commodities—that Whole Foods rooftop was the only place anyone could park on a Friday night in October, in D.C., in 2023.

The androgynous king turns into the alley like a size-inclusive model dominating a Milan runway. Outfitted in a black jumpsuit cataphract with a canyon plunge neckline. Two tiny, silver chains bridge the chasm of skin. Platform heel combat boots and a short cape affixed to their shoulders, midnight-shimmer fabric. It billows in the incessant city wind. Wide-brimmed fedora as their crown—the kind bestowed down iridescent decades to anti-gender essentialists to wear and work. Imur remembers the dozens of names taped, paper-clipped, and glued to the portraits of their mothers from the Indus Valley to Lesbos to Naumkeag lands to the Amazon forest and beyond. Each of Imur's ear piercings is a vow against the continued burning of witches. Nose ring a condemnation of crown-sanctioned theft. Imur struts

Toward sin. Arrives at a door marked like a landlord's cheap secret. They are unapologetic as Catholic guilt. Their knocking on the door, an orgy. The password: ancient carnation. Magic words open the spiral stairway down into a jazz-rattling basement. Imur flows into the miniature foyer in the den of the Mother of Blues. It was here, last week, when Joan Crawford asked if Imur the young androgynous king knew: did Miss Josephine Baker suck on Frida Kahlo's bottom lip like crystallized honey, that one night in the umpteenth hour of the 1930s? The king was clueless

Until now; they squeeze now around the painter and performer on the stairs, seven steps from the top, twined mid-demonstration. Imur smears on by as strokes of acrylic paint lick Baker's canvas of cheek. Imur trickles toward the pleasure sea sublimated into a history of queer bodies. The brass song transitions. *Bad Romance* is the next

Invitation. The androgynous king shatters the threshold with their red carpet entrance. They lift their hat and nod their fresh glacier-glazed hair tips to their contemporaries. Mom Chung lifts a glass. At the speakeasy bar,

Oscar Wilde pours the nectar of forbidden fruit into a cocktail shaker. Dickinson guards a barstool seat for Susan, who's in the bathroom here, not at her husband's house. Bayard Rustin perches on the bar counter, here to defy functional fixedness and straight-washing. James Baldwin and Langston Hughes, among many others, Charleston like any other Dick and Jane

Testing the temperature of compatibility with sweat-slick dance. From the midsection of the grenadine-redolent bar, Virginia Woolf drains her old fashioned then drags a tuxedoed Vita to the dance floor deluge. With a re-hearsed delivery, Mercedes de Acosta approaches the pseudo-Ptolemaic queen Rose Cleveland by the crisp, blaring brass band—*How much kissing can Cleopatra stand?* Mercedes attempts to pass it off as casual curiosity. Atop a corner table, Indya Moore scatters sequin waves with their twirling. Androgynous King makes like the next chapter in a saga and stitches them-selves among & along the violets. Imur lifts their hat like a god-damn queen

During a knighting and, at random, selects Hans Christian Andersen's bob-bing head as its crown. Imur accepts a bedazzled astronaut's helmet from Sir Elton John and reinvents the Bernie Lean. Willi Ninja drops into a split for queer-kind. The house lights the floor neon lemon. Even if the landlord cuts the lights, the friends of Dorothy keep dancing.

WELCOME TO THE GRAND VIEW

CHANLEE LUU

Hannah said "that's a light-yellow chick,
    not a *bright* yellow chick,"
      your pencil brushing the paper
        as we colored in our hopes,
          our incubated eggs waiting for daylight.

You have always been too frail. Our chick never made a peep.

Hannah is a palindrome, so was eye.
    Though you told no one, being a nun
      was on your distant radar.
        No, this was not a case of religion,
          but one of light. You dimmed ourselves
            each eve to someone more studious.

Hannah is a palindrome, so is aha.
Never had you read a girl rendered so inquisitive.
Never had you known desire so green.
Never had you heard a voice so sure.
But it was years before ours hatched.

You have always been a mystery. Our blade of grass dewed in the night.

In high school, we pondered the reversal of names.
Eelnahc plummeted you into the deep sea—
solo menacing creature
slinking through the currents
primed for centuries of sagas,
each eve growing new barnacles.
Loch Ness defied. Eel ew yêu.
Disgust transfigured into love.

17

Hannah is a palindrome, so is civic.

A case of duty refiled into a case of daring.

A tunic and veil resewed into a coat of arms.

A kayak soaring the surface before a grand canyon.

Hannah is a palindrome, but you are not.

So when you smile at the sight of a beautiful

girl, let the rush of awe fill you with joy

instead of fear. Let it be yellow,

bold and breathless. Let it be a palindrome,

so no one mistakes it when they

try to read it backwards.

FROZEN

BREE FRAM

In the first month of the Trump administration, a profound and insidious chill has settled over many communities, particularly those already marginalized. A day 1 executive order purported to ensure the federal government and taxpayer dollars would not be used to "unconstitutionally abridge the free speech of any American citizen," but has had the opposite effect.[1] Hate has been emboldened; pride in anything about who we are, other than the administration's view of American exceptionalism, has been silenced. The early actions of the administration sent shockwaves through public discourse, freezing speech, impeding action, and stalling personal growth. Whether through fear of retaliation, the erasure of historical truths, or the psychological weight of living under a government perceived as hostile, countless individuals found themselves paralyzed. This chilling effect has left many frozen in place, uncertain of how to proceed.

People hesitate to show support, even in the smallest ways, for anything the Trump administration opposes. I have received private messages from people who confided that they were afraid to like or comment on something I shared on social media, fearing that visibility might make them a target. This self-censorship is not mere paranoia; it is a response to an administration that, from the outset, showed a willingness to attack dissenters. When people fear engaging in basic discourse, democracy itself suffers. Public participation—essential for progress and change—becomes stifled, leaving voices unheard and issues unaddressed.

Beyond personal fear, a broader institutional suppression of knowledge became evident with the administration's actions. Does removal of all references to transgender people from government websites[2], a list of forbidden words in research publications.[3] Or does pulling books from library shelves sound like the actions of an administration focused on free speech? These erasures were not accidental; they were deliberate attempts to rewrite reality, to render certain identities invisible in the present and the past. Schools at Ft. Campbell pulled books off the shelf that mentioned slavery and civil rights.[4] The Department of Defense schools on Ft. Campbell and across the South exist in part because Southern states once refused to educate the children of Black soldiers after desegregation was mandated. Now, those same schools are purging the very history that explains their existence. Such erasures send a clear message: some histories, some identities, are inconvenient to those in power and are therefore expendable.

The impact of this erasure is profound. When a government actively removes historical truths and marginalized identities from public discourse, it asserts dominance—a declaration that only certain narratives deserve recognition. The chilling effect here extends beyond policy; it permeates the psyche. If history is erased, if communities are rendered invisible, then their struggles, their victories, and their continued existence become precarious. It is an attempt to erase not just the past but the possibility of a different future.

The psychological toll of such an environment cannot be overstated. One message I received from a NASA employee speaks to this directly. They expressed fear in merely opening their work email, dreading another administrative directive reaffirming compliance with Trump's executive orders. The weight of such an existence—constantly on edge, perpetually afraid—prevents people from thriving. Instead, they become locked in survival mode, focused only on navigating the next day, the next hour, without daring to dream beyond their immediate reality. For many in the transgender community, and for other marginalized groups, this is not just political rhetoric; it is life under siege.

To understand the horrors of warfare, learning what happens to a population under siege is a good place to start. We're seeing a modern-day example right now. Locked in place, survival resources dwindling, and the constant stress of wondering where the next attack will come from, take an immense toll. Transgender people denied passports that reflect their gender are trapped in the United States.[5] Health care is fading away as hospitals and insurers focus on government dollars instead of patient care.[6] As corporations supported by government contracts withdraw their dollars from marginalized communities, services shrink.[7] As the resource pool shrinks, competition intensifies, and infighting can threaten to tear communities apart from the inside. Without relief, the siege unbroken, the end result is a withering away of the population and a fracturing of what bound them together.

Mental health professionals understand this freeze, especially when prolonged, to be toxic. Frozen in a state of heightened stress, tension, and hyperarousal, the body suffers real long-term damage.[8] On a personal level, I've also felt this paralysis. My growth has stalled, my ability to learn stunted by unrelenting crisis response. When every moment is consumed by reacting to threats, there is no room for curiosity, no space for intellectual expansion. Every book I pick up is interrupted by thoughts of writing another to-do list. I don't have the bandwidth to check in on friends, and I'm constantly aware of how easy it would be to lash out in anger. Supporting a community under threat consumes all available energy. It is a cruel irony: those most in need of strength and resilience are drained by the very fight for survival.

But if fear is the freeze, then hope must be the antifreeze. Hope is not naive optimism; it is the radical act of believing in a better future despite overwhelming adversity. It is found in the quiet resistance of those who continue to speak even when their voices shake. It is in the messages from strangers, seeking comfort and finding solidarity. It is in the act of remembering history, of refusing to let the past be erased, of ensuring that stories of struggle and resilience are passed on.

Hope is also in the choice to persist. Even in the face of fear, engaging—whether through conversation, education, or advocacy—thaws the ice that seeks to immobilize us. Every time someone defies the pressure to remain silent, they contribute to a collective warmth that can melt the suppressive frost. Every act of existence, no matter how small, is an assertion of humanity against those who seek to erase it.

The first month of the Trump administration casts a dark, chilling shadow on the coming years. But even in the coldest winters, warmth persists. It persists in the stories we tell, in the truths we refuse to let die, in the communities we build and protect. The antidote to fear is not only hope—it is courage, actively cultivated, relentlessly pursued. So speak, use the rights you've been given, by birth or by choice, and stand up for the rights of every American. And with enough truly free speech, we will thaw what has been frozen and move forward once more, with memory intact and hearts open.

The views presented here are personal and do not reflect the official guidance or position of the United States government or the Department of Defense.

[1]www.whitehouse.gov/presidential-actions/2025/01/restoring-freedom-of-speech-and-ending-federal-censorship

[2]www.npr.org/2025/02/14/stonewall-monument-transgender-park-service

[3]www.kpbs.org/news/economy/2025/02/07/federal-list-of-forbidden-words-may-jeopardize-research-at-ucsd

[4]www.clarksvillenow.com/local/books-mentioning-slavery-civil-rights-removed-from-shelves-at-fort-campbell-schools/

[5] www.vox.com/politics/399502/transgender-passports-lgbtq-trump-marco-rubio-travel-gender

[6]www.usatoday.com/story/news/health/2025/02/04/transgender-hospitals-gender-affirming-care

[7]www.them.us/story/human-rights-campaign-layoffs-restructuring-lgbtq-rights-organization

[8]www.nicabm.com/topic/trauma-responses

GANYMEDE

JONATHAN HARPER

Tyler Addison, age eight, aspiring archaeologist, lover of mythology, was the only child left unattended at the Johnson's cocktail party. While the other children had gone down to the basement playroom hours ago, Tyler had instead slipped away. He was always doing this: disappearing in plain sight. It wasn't that he disliked the others, but they were a different type of children. They were loud and rough and sometimes mean; Tyler had never been any good at the games they liked to play.

Instead, he had hidden himself in Mr. Johnson's study, where he could read in peace. He had brought his favorite book, a large compendium of Greek myths, tattered with earmarked pages; he never went anywhere without it. He had studied this book and considered himself quite the expert. He could recite entire epics of the Greek gods and heroes to anyone who cared to listen.

He had been alone for what felt like hours when two adults came stumbling into the office, breathless and giggling, hands rubbing against each other. The man was whispering something into her ear when they noticed him sitting there.

The lady gave out a gasp. "What are you doing in here?" Instantly, her friend wrapped his arms around her waist as if trying to redirect her out of the room. "You shouldn't sneak up on people like that," she said.

"Oh, he's fine. Let's leave him alone," the man said as he pulled her out of the room.

It was almost ten o'clock, and as they left, Tyler let out a heavy sigh, closed his book, and wandered out to find his father.

The partygoers were all in the same stages of affectionate inebriation. They draped themselves over the long couches, leaning against each other, swaying in place as they laughed and smoked with their cavernous mouths. Music flowed in loud beats that made the abandoned cheese plates tremble on their stands. And there, among them, was his father, Charles Addison, newfound bachelor, landscape architect, savvy mastermind of the annual botanical roadshow, making a spectacle of himself.

He sat on the chaise lounge, having liberated Mrs. Johnson's foot from her shoe and rubbed it tenderly between his fingers while she laughed into her wine glass. It was so odd seeing his father like this, grinning devilishly as he brought her big toe up to his mouth and kissed it gently. They were so consumed in each other that no one noticed Tyler wander in and sit down on the large ottoman in the corner, book resting on his lap.

Just as Tyler was ready to sink into a pitiful mood, he was suddenly aware of movement in the hallway. Emerging from the basement was Madeline Johnson, the young lady of the house, dressed in her purple gown that swished regally around her. She walked into the center of the parlor, her expression guarded as she surveyed the party and, without hesitation, plopped down beside him.

"So, this is where you've been hiding," she said.

Suddenly, the whole room was aware of their presence. Even Charles, wide-eyed, dropped his hostess's foot and went scrabbling for a nearby plate.

"Madeline, dear," her mother said. "What are you doing up here?"

"It's getting late," she said drolly. "Everyone's falling asleep."

"But the night is young!" Charles said as he popped a cherry tomato into his mouth. But Mrs. Johnson ignored her. Instead, she turned to Tyler. "Are you having a fun time?"

"He hasn't been down all night," Madeline replied.

"I'm ready to go home," he muttered.

"He's tired. We all are."

"Oh, Madeline, go entertain him for a bit," Mr. Johnson said. "He shouldn't be by himself."

But Madeline crossed her arms. "I'm not a babysitter."

"I don't need a babysitter," Tyler grumbled.

"Oh, perhaps you're hungry. Maybe you would like a snack?" Mrs. Johnson clasped her hands together like a bishop to a chorus of agreements from behind her.

In *The Odyssey*, Circe fed sailors a feast that turned them into swine. Tyler imagined the guests eating from the plates before violently changing. He thought that would bring this vile party to a halt.

Instead, Madeline calmly rose, took him by the hand and led him out of the parlor as the adults laughed on behind them.

*

Upstairs, Madeline's room was like a palace in the clouds. Everything was light and airy. Fluffy cream rug, walls painted like a sunset, strings of fairy lights hung from the ceiling. It was the most beautiful room Tyler had ever seen. And then, his eyes flickered to the oversized bookcase where an entire menagerie of ponies stood smiling down at him. They were fat and multi-colored with bright hair that sparkled.

"Do you like my horses?" Madeline asked. She sat at the small vanity, watching him through the mirror.

"You sure have a lot."

She sighed. "This summer, I'm going to horse camp. I'm going to learn dressage. Do you know what that is?" Tyler did not. "It's horseback riding. I'm going to learn to ride horses for competition." She seemed very proud to say this.

Sheepishly, Tyler inspected the toy ponies and pulled one from the shelf. It was lime green with a blue mane. He thought it looked the most boyish out of the bunch.

"You can play with them if you want," Madeline offered. She retrieved a toy barn from the closet and pulled another horse from the shelf. It was the color of peaches with purple hair that sparkled under the light. "But, you can't use Lavender. She's my favorite. How about this one?" She handed him a more traditional horse figurine. It was a brown stallion with dark plastic hair. "I call him Mustard. He's the strongest of them all."

They lined up all the horses into a long parade. The Lavender pony minded the foals in the barn, observing from a distance, while Tyler moved Mustard around to keep the other horses in line. They were journeying back to the barn with fresh supplies for the babies, and all were in danger of getting lost, especially the green pony, who had a habit of wandering off. Whenever it became separated from the group, Mustard was then charged with assembling the search party.

It didn't take long for Madeline to abandon the game. She announced Lavender would serve as lookout and crawled up onto the puffy cloud of the bed. Soon, Tyler realized she was no longer playing. Instead, she was watching him, studying him as if he were a puzzle with pieces that did not fit neatly together. Her gaze was so intense it felt like a ray of heat against the back of his neck. He placed Mustard down and reopened his book. He didn't even want to think of the ponies anymore, even if they were all around him, staring up with their painted smiles.

"What's your book about?" she finally asked. Her face was inquisitive, welcoming. Whatever weirdness he had felt was gone. He crawled up next to her and watched her turn each page, skimming over the contents. He kept waiting for her to ask questions and test his knowledge, and he was filled with disappointment when she put it down.

"Let me show my favorite one," he said. He thumbed through to the right chapter and laid it out. "It's the story of Ganymede. Zeus favored him, so he turned himself into an Eagle and swooped down and brought him to Olympus."

"Favored?" she asked. "What does that mean?"

"The gods picked certain mortals to reward. He was one of them."

"Why?"

"Because he was beautiful and kind. So, Zeus made him a cupbearer," Tyler said with pride.

Madeline gave him a hard look. "That's it?"

"Well, Zeus also gave him eternal youth. He got to stay a boy forever," he said dreamily.

"Sounds creepy."

"Oh." His chest deflated like a balloon. "Well, there are other good stories, too."

"Tell me one," she said with a yawn.

Tyler began recounting the tales of Olympus, though he soon realized Madeline had fallen asleep. As he stared around the room, he felt himself sink into the comforter, his eyes drifting over the soft pastel colors and cloudy shapes around him.

Somewhere in the twilight hours, when the reasonable world was fast asleep and traveling through their dreams, Tyler crossed the bridge back into the waking world. At first, he sat there in a haze, eyes adjusting to the dark around him. There was a pillow nestled under his head and a blanket covering him. And then, it all came clear: he was still lying on the edge of Madeline's bed. There she was, sleeping soundly under the covers. It was so quiet, startling quiet. And then came the sudden realization: the party was long over, and for some reason, he was still there.

Almost instantly, the tears began to well up in his eyes. Where was his father? Had he been left behind? As the first sob started, he could feel Madeline rustle in place, so he clasped his hands over his mouth to muffle the noise. The last thing he wanted was for her to wake up and find him crying.

But no, he knew his father wouldn't have left him. Tyler knew this, knew that he must be there still in the house. There was no point in going back to sleep. He was morbidly awake and turning angry. Quietly, he rose out from under the blanket and tiptoed out of the room. He felt brave now, determined. Once he found his father, he would shake him awake, and they would drive home.

The rest of the house was dark and gloomy. Only a few steps down the stairs, he could see the emptiness of the front parlor. He called out into the darkness in the loudest whisper he could muster, but there was no response. He called out again before moving back up to the long hallway of the second floor, where Madeline still slept blissfully. He tried the other doors: a bathroom, a linen closet, an empty guest-room where the bed was still made.

At the end of the hall, he pushed open the large double doors, wincing as they creaked. It was a large bedroom, delicately laid out with fancy furnishing and soft drapes. In the middle of the room sat a large four-post bed, partially illuminated by the window. He willed himself to be invisible, his footsteps barely touched the carpet as he crept inside, and there he saw the three of them together. Mrs. Johnson was curled up in his father's arms while Mr. Johnson was nestled against his father's back, the three of them linked in a strange chain.

He stood there a moment, studying them, how their bodies melded together so neatly, as if it was the most natural thing in the world. Mr. Johnson's arm gripped his father so tightly as if to prevent him from slipping away. Only then did Tyler realize he was not supposed to be there.

He crept back out and closed the door, which snapped shut. Fearful they'd wake, he dashed back down the hall and crawled on the edge of Madeline's bed, pulling the blanket over him and waited patiently, but no one came. For the rest of the night, he lay there on the edge of sleep, wondering what he had seen and if it was all just a dream.

*

In the early morning, their parents stood watching them sleep. "Aren't they darling?" Mrs. Johnson said in her honey-sweet voice.

Charles agreed and watched Tyler's eyes twitch gently as he breathed. His son was somewhere else, always drifting into another world he didn't fully understand. He leaned down and carefully lifted him up.

"Don't forget his book," Mr. Johnson said.

"Of course not. He'd kill me if I did."

*

Tyler felt himself placed in the passenger seat of his father's sedan, still wrapped in his blanket. From the corner of his eye, he was sure he saw his father kiss them both, a quick peck on the lips. The sky was turning that light pink of early morning as they drove out of the city.

"You awake, buddy?" Charles asked, and Tyler looked up at him. "Do you want breakfast?"

He shook his head; he wasn't very hungry.

"Did you have a nice time last night?" his father asked.

"It was ok."

"What would you say if we went back next weekend? Would that be fun?" his father smiled brightly as if everything was wonderful.

Eventually, they pulled into the familiar stretch of their neighborhood. There, at the end of the driveway, perched on the branches of the old maple tree, was a large bird. A hawk, maybe? An eagle?

"You and Madeline could have another sleepover," his father was saying. "We'll order pizza and watch movies, and you can stay up as long as you like."

As he stepped out of the car, Tyler was certain the bird was watching them. It looked majestic, almost mystical. And then, his father slammed the car door shut, and the bird spread its wings. Tyler instantly knew what was going to happen: It would nosedive down and grasp him in his claws and carry him away. He closed his eyes and waited, a tiny smile on his lips.

But when he opened them, he was still there, and the bird was gone.

NEGATIVE SPACE

SUZANNE FELDMAN

Mark's mother left a message on his landline while he was at work. Mark took off his coat and threw his keys into the blue plastic bowl on the kitchen table. He already knew what the message was, as though her words were being transmitted by the flashing red light in some kind of old-woman code. Even though he knew, he tapped the play button.

If you want any of your father's things, said her voice, rough from cigarettes, not grief, come over before I throw everything away.

It was raining outside and getting colder. It might even snow, but that didn't matter. Mark put on his wet coat, pocketed his keys, and went out to the car.

His father had died six days ago, near Eugene, in Oregon, and late last week, the new wife, now a widow, had called the old wife to let her know. New wife was taking care of the funeral arrangements and had even offered to pay their airfare from Maryland. It was a nice gesture, as his mother said, but neither of them had any intention of spending five or six hours on a plane just to make sure the old bastard was deep in the ground and covered up with dirt.

Mark backed out of his driveway, turned on the windshield wipers, and headed for his mother's house, five miles away. His father had left when he was eleven. Like, just fucking left. It wasn't even a classic move—I'm going out for cigarettes. He'd disappeared one Thursday morning. Gone to work, supposedly, but actually, he'd taken the car and driven away. Driven away! His mother never even called the police. She was glad he was gone. When Mark came home from school that day, his mother told him how things were going to be.

We're never going to hear from him. Anything you want to say about him, say it right now—ask any questions. Because we're never going to talk about him, ever again.

What kind of questions does an eleven-year-old kid have in those kind of circumstances? He hadn't asked, Why did he leave us? He knew why. Dad couldn't hold a job, and he drank. Dad was a drunk who painted beautiful pictures.

The paintings—all landscapes—were dreamlike. Heavy clouds hung over trees losing their leaves in dark murmurations. Under the clouds, his father used a flat blue housepaint for the sky. For grass, cheap tempera— chalky green and thick. Still, in Mark's mind, the paintings were beautiful, and because of this, he'd thought his father had a beautiful soul.

In high school, he learned to paint in art class—his father

wouldn't teach him. He watched his teacher brush dark blue watercolor over wet paper. Every time a drop of color touched the wet surface, it burst into a flower shape. The teacher, a young woman with glasses and utterly black hair, picked up the paper by its edges and tipped it gently, guiding the water over the page, letting the flower shapes run out of themselves, streaking the page with color. When his teacher set the paper on the table again, Mark examined her, the way he examined his father when he was painting in the spare bedroom. She had glanced up, ready to explain this technique to the class, but her eyes met his before she could say anything. Instead of speaking, she'd looked down at the painting again, and that was when he saw the tenderness in her face—for paint on wet paper—that he had never seen in his father.

Mark's mother still lived in the house where he'd grown up, a split-level with azaleas clustered around the front porch. She'd dug up most of the front yard in the fall after Mark's father left. She'd planted everything she could find that would flower in the spring, and in the spring, her yard was the first to bloom. Now, in winter, the mulch looked thin and there was no color except for the beige siding on her house. Mark unlocked the front door and walked in to find his mother sitting on the couch in the living room, smoking.

"You're here," she said.

"Are you okay?" he asked.

His mom looked up at him with her emotionless grey eyes. "Never been better."

She didn't want to talk about dad. Fine. He took off his coat and hung it in the bathroom where it could drip dry.

"Look on the dining table," said his mom, still smoking.

Mark went into the dining room and saw the paint box at the head of the table where no one ever sat now. The box was like a wooden briefcase in its size and shape, the light wood stained with oily residues. A bed of newspaper protected the table. The box's familiarity made him blink. The smell of oil paint, turpentine, and linseed oil came back to him in a weird rush. The spare bedroom came back to him, vivid, with summer sun coming through the window, a radio tuned to a classical station. On the easel, another landscape. He remembered his father turning to smile at him, then reach for his bottle. The memory was strong, like a taste. Mark pushed his tongue against his teeth and went back into the living room.

"Don't you want it?" said his mother. "You like to paint."

"I have a paint box," said Mark. "I have paint. I have everything." He took his paints out once or twice a year. His paintings weren't good because he didn't practice. He'd never showed them to anyone but his mother. She'd picked out one she liked and taken it home. He didn't know where it was now. She'd never put it up on a wall.

"Well then," said his mother, "you can take it and throw it into a dumpster."

"Why is it even still in the house?" said Mark. He sat next to her on the couch, took the cigarette from between her fingers and stubbed it out.

She gave him an irritated look. "Will you get me another one from my purse?"

"No," he said.

His mother got up and came back with an open pack of Salems. "I want you to have it," said his mother. She sat down again, tapped the pack on the coffee table, but didn't take another cigarette out. "I can't even stand looking at it."

So, you're giving me something to hate. He didn't say that. "I'll take care of it."

"You're a good son," she said, flat, like always. "Have you eaten?"

"I just got home from work."

"I'll fix something." She pushed herself off the couch and went into the kitchen.

Mark stayed where he was. He reached for the remote and turned on the TV. The local news came on, reporting, as usual, nothing but death, destruction, and the weather. He muted the TV and watched without any sound. A building burned behind spectators who spoke into the microphone. He listened to his mother opening and closing cabinets. He smelled butter in a frying pan. On TV, someone bit into a juicy hamburger. Mark leaned forward, hands between his knees, and watched until the next commercial came on. Then he got up and went into the dining room.

The paint box. Mark pulled out the chair but didn't sit. He'd sat in this chair before of course. When he was a kid, he'd thought the chair might give him some kind of power, though he was never sure what kind, or even why he would want the power of a runaway dad.

Mark sat down in his father's chair. Any special power was long gone. That felt true. But the box.

One autumn weekend, when Mark was nine or ten, his father put the box in a backpack he was taking to the mountains in the western part of the state. Mark had begged to go with him. Fine, but you can't talk to me while I'm painting. I'm in the Zone. Understand?

In the car, on the way to the mountains, his father turned on a classical station. Mark knew most of the composers his dad liked. "That's Dvorak," he'd said.

"Nope. Guess again."

Mark listened closely.

"It's Smetana, of course," said his father impatiently.

Mark hesitated. He knew the piece, and it was Dvorak. "Oh. Yeah."

"Obviously," said his father, frowning. "Listen to that static," he said, and turned the music off before the announcer could come on to tell them that it was Dvorak.

In the silence, Mark remembered looking out the window at a row of poplars flashing past the car, their leaves glittering in the morning sun. He'd been at the age when life reveals itself, and he suddenly realized he had no idea how to argue with his dad. His mother couldn't do it without raising her voice, which made his father yell at her. Mark didn't want any yelling. He didn't say anything for the rest of the drive, but he fumed over being right and not being able to say so.

They stopped at a trailhead in a state park, deep in the September woods. Mark's father shouldered the backpack and tucked an aluminum easel under his arm.

"You're going hike with all that?" said Mark. "How far are we going?"

"'Half a league, half a league, half a league onward!'" sang his father. "Close the trunk." He tossed Mark the keys. "If you get bored you can come back here and wait in the car."

"I won't get bored," said Mark.

They hiked for an hour before they stopped at a sign that said, *Scenic View*.

"This'll do," said his father. He set the backpack down carefully and unfolded the metal easel. He pulled a blank canvas out of the pack and then the paintbox. Mark sat on a rock. The view of the valley looked scenic enough. He was hungry and found himself wondering how long this landscape would take. His father spent hours and hours alone in the spare bedroom.

"Did you bring your lunch?" asked his father.

"No," said Mark.

"Why'd you leave it in the car? Now you're gonna have to walk for an hour before you can eat." His father wasn't looking at him, busy setting up his palette and brushes. His tone was offhand, as though the idea of lunch had just occurred to him.

"Mom didn't make me anything."

His father reached into the depths of the backpack and

pulled out a crushed peanut butter sandwich in a plastic bag. "Me neither."

"But I didn't make anything," said Mark. "I don't have lunch."

"That wasn't very smart." His father practically threw the sandwich at him. Mark just caught it. "Eat the whole thing," said his dad. "And leave me alone."

He'd turned his back to Mark, the sandwich, the car keys.

Now, sitting in his chair at the dining table, Mark remembered the view of the valley, the crushed sandwich in his hand and the stark understanding that he was of no use to his father. He never had been. He'd walked all the way back to the car and when he got to the trailhead, he dropped the sandwich into the first trash can he saw. Their car was alone in the parking area. He'd opened the driver's door and sat behind the steering wheel. Even at nine or ten, he could reach the pedals. There was half a tank of gas. Where did he want to go?

Instead of driving away, Mark put his hand on the horn and pushed. In the warm afternoon, the horn bleated into the forest. The noise rose into the air and floated up the mountain to where his father was painting. The landscape was probably almost done. Finishing, with a house paint blue sky and caked-on green for grass, would be done in the spare bedroom.

And, Mark remembered, for the first time, he had realized that his father's work was ugly. That if painting was a way for him to show his soul, then his soul was ugly. Mark took his hand off the horn, climbed into the back seat, curled up on the torn vinyl upholstery and shut his eyes. After another hour and a half, his father returned. Mark listened as he put his equipment in the trunk. The trunk slammed shut and his father got behind the wheel. The key was already in the ignition. Without saying anything at all, his father started the car. Mark waited for him to ask are you asleep? Are you okay? Or even, Did you eat the whole sandwich? Instead, in silence, his father pulled onto the main road. After a long time, he turned on the classical station, which, Mark realized, was still playing Dvorak because it was the composer's birthday.

Mark put his hands on the table, flat, on either side of the wooden box. It was bulky, banged-up thing. Without opening it, he knew there were brushes and crinkled-up tubes of paint inside, a palette caked with dried-up oils. His own paint box, in contrast, still smelled new. His oil paints had barely been used. His brushes, which were expensive, were clean. He always scraped down his own palette when he was done painting, even though his father's voice, inside

Mark's head, said what a waste. Mark had never, ever used house paint. It's cheaper. Looks the same. "No, it doesn't," he said now, in a low voice so his mother couldn't hear him.

In his mind, his father laughed.

Mark's own work was clunky and he knew it. The still lives he set up so carefully—beautiful blue bottles and perfect apples on a flowered tablecloth—looked forced. He'd attempted portraits but stopped when he turned to the mirror and tried to paint himself. His father's mouth and eyebrows looked back at him, and he had to stop. Mark had never painted landscapes. Had no interest.

Was it like Pandora, he wondered, hands still on either side of the box.

His mother came into the dining room, wiping her hands on a kitchen towel. "What's wrong?"

"This fucking box."

"Honey," she said. "Throw it out if you don't want it."

"I don't want it."

"Then throw it out," she said in a tone that said it didn't matter to her what he did.

"I want to open it," he said, but she'd gone into the kitchen.

In a minute, he heard her shaking a colander full of hot spaghetti.

Mark bit the insides of his cheeks. He put his hand on the box. Two little rusting hooks held it shut. With his thumb, he pushed one out of its metal loop.

"Dinner's ready," said his mother. "You want to eat at the kitchen table?"

He pushed the other hook out of its loop. "Yeah."

"Come and get it."

Mark took a breath through his teeth and opened the box.

"Do you want parmesan?"

Inside there was nothing. No crinkled tubes, no brushes. Only the caked palette was there, piled with globs of dried blue house paint. Mark closed the box. He got up and went into the kitchen where the air was steamy.

"Where's his paint? Where's all his stuff?"

His mother forked pasta onto his plate, handed it to him and sat. "I threw it away."

Mark stood holding his plate. "There was nothing I could've used?"

"What about the palette?"

Mark sat down. "It's useless. It's..."

His mother twirled spaghetti against a spoon. "He was trash, Mark. He was trash and that's what he left us."

Mark stared at his dinner. Sometimes he'd tried to imagine their courtship. His father's charm somehow casting a shadow over his mother's iron endurance. "What did you see in him?"

His mother sighed and put her fork down. "Mark," she said. "You're a good son. You got his best qualities. Or maybe you didn't. Maybe they're my best qualities. Now let's talk about something else. How's work? Who are you seeing these days?"

"Nobody," said Mark.

"Well, that just isn't healthy," said his mother.

She was about to say more, he could tell. He pushed his chair back and stood.

His mother looked up, eyes wide. "Where're you going?"

"I'm going to the bathroom," said Mark.

His mother hunched in her chair, as though she hadn't meant for him to see that.

Mark went into the bathroom and shut the door. He turned on the bathroom fan, which was loud and annoying, and sat on the edge of the tub. He took out his cell phone and scrolled through his contacts.

Dad. Listed there with everyone else.

Mark had never called his dad. He had no idea if the number still worked or if new wife had had the presence of mind to deactivate the phone.

He wondered if she would answer if he called.

Mark clenched his teeth together and tapped the number. In a moment, the phone rang, far away in Oregon. It occurred to Mark that perhaps his father was currently resting in a funeral parlor, or perhaps even a crematorium, and his phone was ringing.

You got me. Leave a message.

In Maryland and alive, Mark blinked. He took a breath. He wanted to say the most hurtful thing he could think of, but nothing seemed hurtful enough to leave as a message for someone who would never hear it. He waited until he could feel the voicemail getting ready to hang up on his silence.

Finally, he said, "We never loved you either."

TO BE BLACK AND GAY AND FEMININE

an excerpt from the memoir-in-progress *Pink Black Boy*
(Inspired by "Young, Gifted and Black" by Nina Simone and
"To Be Black and Woman and Alive" by Crystal Valentine and
Aaliyah Jihad)

PIÉRRE RAMON THOMAS

To be a Black man and gay and feminine is to understand that society holds no space for you to exist peacefully. You might create small oases where you're fully free to express yourself and exist without judgment, but you're not afforded the full freedom others have. *Not unless you advocate for yourself.* If you're not accosted by the Bible-thumpers condemning you to an eternal lake of fire on one side, you're harangued by the "pro-black," Pan-Africanist hoteps and hoteptresses who peddle "Being gay isn't African; you learned that from the white man!" on the other side. If you're not dealing with racism from straight *and* queer Whites on one side, you're dealing with the femme-phobic, masc4masc bros *within* the LGBTQ+ community on the other side. You experience these forms of hatred many times back-to-back, and still, you must embody resilience.

To be a Black man and gay and feminine is to have your sexuality and gender expression easily recognized, and because your sexuality and gender expression are easily recognizable, you often have to endure hatred from people you're supposed to share community with. On the other hand, Black gay masculine men are able to traipse through the Black community unseen and unharmed because, even in the twenty-first century, people *still* associate male femininity with homosexuality—not understanding that gender expression has nothing to do with sexuality. (Look at Rick James and Prince, for example.) Anyone—masculine or feminine, man or woman—can be gay, bisexual, or straight. So, because Black gay masculine men are able to have their sexuality unnoticed, undetected, and unseen, they often join in on the verbal violence and judgment against Black gay feminine men *with* the Black community at large. Instead of forming community with Black gay feminine men or acknowledging that we're part of the same larger community, Black gay masculine men make it clear that we are not in community with each other and encourage others to detest us, deride us, and consider us unlovable.

To be a Black man and gay and feminine is *to know* and *have the understanding* that there is not a premium among gay men for feminine men, especially *Black* feminine men. When femininity *is* desired in a man, it's usually in white, Latino, or Asian men. Black gay feminine men are an afterthought or not thought of at all. A *nonthought*. Masculine men say, "If I wanted to be with a girl, I'd just be with a girl" or "We're men. We're supposed to act like men." Even other feminine men say, "Girl, I don't wanna be with no other femme; I don't want to bump pocketbooks." Sometimes, you are rejected and undesired for both your Blackness *and* your femininity, and, at other times, your femininity as a Black man is somehow considered contradictory or oxymoronic. It is to know this and see this and *still* love yourself enough to be yourself anyway.

To be a Black man and gay and feminine is to know that, to many, you're not considered worthy enough to become a romantic partner. Since *very few* are willing to love a Black gay feminine man out in the open, you must be willing to be "loved" in secret. To the fearful majority, a Black gay feminine man is good enough for sex, good enough to satisfy that secret desire they have of being with a feminine man— especially if they date a woman publicly—but a Black gay feminine man is *not* considered good enough to be loved and claimed publicly. Knowing this forces you to choose: Will you continue to be used secretly or wait for someone willing to love you publicly?

To be a Black man and gay and feminine is to know that, friend-wise, you don't hold a lot of value in the imaginations of women unless you are the comic relief, the one with "all the tea," the one who can "clock all the DLs," or you can provide some service only a gay man can provide. At best, you're a poodle: there for her companionship. When she's in the mood, she plays with you, but when she has what she needs, she leaves you to yourself—even if you're in need of her companionship. At worst, the "friendship" is transparently one-sided. She cries and vents to you about her man troubles. You're there to make sure her hair, makeup, and outfits are on point. Her proximity to you ensures that she can partake in the crazy party life of the gays—but you can never seek depth or intimacy from her because "the friendship" never goes deeper than that. Hell! When you try to seek some measure of reciprocity in "the friendship," suddenly, like a magician, she disappears. She's nowhere to be found. She's busy. And God forbid you are an unconventional gay: not into makeup or hair or fashion or celebrity gossip; not really that heavy into partying; spiritual; artsy; into nature and plants and herbs and gardening; prefers museums, plays, art shows, movies, and unconventional events. If you are different from the caricature they have in their minds of what a gay man is, you lose your value to them as a friend.

To be a Black man and gay and feminine is not to have your softness, your delicateness, your tenderness validated. Stereotypically, Black men are supposed to be aggressive, masculine, and threatening. Many have claimed that femininity in Black men is performative and, in most cases, is nothing but a futile attempt to either be *like* Black women or to try to *outdo* Black women. Despite the fact that Black feminine men were once little Black feminine boys, naturally and organically, who also *learned* and *modeled* their femininity after the femininity of their Black mommas, grandmommas, aunts, female cousins, and so on and so forth. (Black male femininity is both naturally occurring *and* reinforced by the Black female presence in their lives.) To their myopic conclusion, however, Black male femininity is fake; to them, there's no way femininity can be expressed from a vessel from which we've come to expect nothing but violence and aggression.

To be a Black man and gay and feminine is to suffer from the negative stereotype that *all* Black gay feminine men are loud, toxic, messy, and catty. What the juvenile nature of that stereotype doesn't acknowledge is that there are a number of Black gay feminine men who are quiet, mature, peaceful, even-tempered, loving, drama-free, and too many other positive traits that I don't have the white space to list. However, it is much easier to regard a subset of people with a generalization rather than getting to know people individually so—

To be a Black man and gay and feminine—unapologetically—is to write a love letter to yourself every day. It is to be a banner, a living example, a walking declaration of self-love.

COMMUNIQUE TO MY 20 SOMETHING SELF

DAN VERA

Hello
It's me
or *you* from the future.
Your future.
Here to tell you you're still alive.

You're living in a place you never considered
a future that seemed as veiled and dark as the dark closet
you cant seem to escape.

Everything you feared never came true.
Or, if it did, it didn't last long.
And somehow, miraculously, you overcame them.
Some of your big questions were answered.
Some, you traded for better questions.
Some exhausted themselves in memory.

Oh yeah, memory became a problem
beginning with memories of you, except
for memories of you which mellowed with time.

You will find it hard to believe things got worse
and better at the same time.

It's perplexing I know, because I'm you.
But it's true.
You learned this the year when Papá almost died.
That very same year in which you also met
the love of your life. Surprise!
I would fear spoilers. But even knowing this,
you will never see it coming.
He will hit you like a ton of the most lovable bricks.
What's better is he will not be a phantom.
You will find a way to make each other laugh
and that laughter will be worth every sad day and
every bleak verse you ever put on your page.
Those pages?
You will keep and revisit them occasionally
to remember that you you were
that you at this minute
reading these words with great disbelief
and bemusement.

MAGICAL THINKING

REGIE CABICO

We all dig our own grave.
All rivers are full of bonfires.
Waterfall tequila in the mind.
Our genesis is alpaca slime
My college drama auditions
were audited by feather dusters.
I get the Olympic medal for the girlie eye roll
A single gem has throbbed in my chest
my whole life till it split
skipping wishing wells
I've been living with a Pyrex heart
Astrology says we get a second partner in life
I want him close as flames
I want this lover to fall for me like confetti
from a Holy Book

FRAMBUESAS SALVAJES

JOSE GUTIERREZ

Al fondo
de tus labios
de frambuesas salvajes
escondes un poema
de amor

Amor,
dejame descubrirte
para probar
la miel sagrada
de tus palabras.

WILD RASPBERRIES

JOSE GUTIERREZ

Deep within
your wild
raspberry lips
you hide
a love poem

Love,
let me discover you
to taste
the sacred honey
of your words.

Translation by Jona Colson

TE QUIERO

JOSE GUTIERREZ

Te dije te quiero
y me oiste
sin escucharme

y mis palabras
fueron libelulas
apasionadas
que volaron
en camara lenta
frente a tu
corazon indiferente
en la grieta de la noche

te dije
te quiero
y nunca
me escuchastes.

I LOVE YOU

JOSE GUTIERREZ

I told you I love you
and you heard me
without listening

and my words
were passionate
dragonflies
that flew
in slow motion
before your
indifferent heart
in the night's rift

I told you
I love you
and you never
listened.

Translation by Jona Colson

I SHOULD HAVE SLEPT WITH THEM ALL: HAIKU

CAROLINE BOCK

Dreams sieve sadness with
desire. Cup my breasts. If I
ache, it's only dawn.

AGAINST IDENTIFICATION

LUKE SUTHERLAND

for Willem Arondeus & Frieda Belinfante

Transsexuals are not cowards
but if you dare look at us
and let "brave" fall from your lips,
don't shrink from any side eye
sizing you up.

Is it brave to desire,
to act on that desire?

Bearing the wet bite
of Amsterdam in March
with bombs in tow, hung
-over from amphetamine
fueled nights of throwing
sand in cogs, a gay rave
by any other name;

the smell of singed cardstock
stuck smartly to the suit collar of a level-headed butch,
or to the wrist of a militantly

flouncing faggot (prelude
to a dead fascist),
tastes better than sex,
feels better than symphony.

There is pleasure in the forge
-ry, of murder sabotaged,
eight hundred thousand
now unidentifiable, still
alive outside the camps—
for now, for today.

Is it desirable to be brave,
to act on that bravery?

Transsexuals are not brave
but necessary, inevitable.
Passports or identity cards,
all documents burn:
write it in my blood
if you must.

MARIGOLD GHAZAL
ALEX CARRIGAN

The one I love stretches out before me like an endless field of marigolds.
They disappear into the sheets, and out bursts the yellow buds of marigolds.

I gently caress each bud that emerges from the plot, but soon my hands
are subsumed by the flourishing of hundreds of newly born marigolds.

I don't have enough time to pick them for bouquets, not enough empty jars
to fill, before the abundance overwhelms me with the scent of marigolds.

I feel myself being pulled into the field, desiring to run my hands over all
the fuzzy buttons until I'm unable to feel my skin deep within the marigolds.

There's no stopping the growth of these flowers, so I decide to simply
allow myself to lay down and let myself become part of the marigolds.

Deep within the field, I can feel my love reach out and embrace me,
and I allow myself to become another plot to grow marigolds.

Perhaps a honeybee will emerge from all the flourishing, but even if we
are no longer found, anyone can come and pick for themselves some marigolds.

SAGE ADVICE

MICHELLE PARKERSON

The juggler

In Eleanor Holmes Norton Park

Levitates allegories:

Some balls drop

Others in rotation

Amid routine fear

daily trepidations

I rehearse:

Expect anything

Stay in practice

Make it look easy

Breathe

(Repeat)

IF I WERE BEING INTERVIEWED BY BEYONCÉ: A PANTOUM

NATALIE E. ILLUM

after Joanna C. Valente

Beyoncé, people tell me I'm not queer enough.
These days, I want to be an avatar. My first girlfriend was high femme.
So bright I had no words for myself. Is *I worship her* a sexuality?
No one who lives here remembers who I kissed in corners. Or daylight.

Maybe I'm an avatar who wanted a trans man.
to prove how split down the middle I was. Bixsexual
in daylight. But even my friends stopped introducing me
because of all that dick, dildo or bio. Erasing me

to prove how split down the middle I was. Bixsexual. Or just Gemini?
No one who lives here remembers loving me in daylight
because of all that dick, inviting me in. Erase.
Who did you say you were? Dyke March or lesbian girlfriend?

No one who lives here remembers inviting me into corners.
Beyoncé, my friends tell me I'm not queer enough. Erased
who I worship. You asked me who I was? Years ago
we were so bright. Now I have no words, no body. Just avatar.

EPHEMERAL

JONA COLSON
(from the Greek, *ephemeros*, lasting or living only a day—
short-lived creatures or insects)

A down-draft of a white cloud, or a frog
diving into the river like a stone.

Maybe something inside—a skipped
heartbeat of a man I tried to kiss.

A mayfly touching her feet to a bay leaf.
Some things are best forgotten.

My father snapping a tomato vine,
close enough for me to see but not cherish.

I am walking hastily to my own extinction
like the luna moth breaking open in rain—

when all my rescues are gone, I'll remember
the pour of milk, a coo of a bird,

my mother's hand waving through glass.

"ON BEING QUEER" OR "THE GAY AGENDA"

DWAYNE LAWSON-BROWN

"They're turning the frogs gay!"
-Alex Jones

I walk into my queer kitchen
Pour a bowl of queer Honey Nut Cherrios
Press the power button on my tiny queer remote control
Open the queer YouTube app
Watch videos by straight artist that go into my queer eyes
As my straight girlfriend comes to kiss my queer cheek
Exiting my queer house into her straight world

I'm locking the door
And everything is normal
The queer toaster still warm from the loafs insertion
The queer floor offering well-worn creaks

I was never straight
Absent minded maybe
A clever rouse played for security
Always knew I wasn't like the other "guys."

FAKE

EVAN O'CONNOR

He said he'd take me back to my metro station, but he stops in front of an apartment building instead. I let him and my shame lead me up, remembering four years ago when I woke up, and it was inescapable. I had been dreaming of a man, the easy certainty of it making me guilty.

Three years ago, when my roommate surprised me by opening my door late at night. He was kind, and tall, and funny, and that night, he was drunk, and giggly, and had broken up with his girlfriend. He complimented me on something, I don't remember, and then we were kissing. We squeezed onto my twin-size mattress and mid-blowjob; he looked up and told me, "I don't think I'm straight," and I laughed so hard we had to stop.

Two years ago, when a friend told me he liked me. His admission warmed me, but I didn't like him back, and that festered until one year ago when I told my friends about my old roommate, and the rejected one asked, "Why didn't you reciprocate?" After I left, he told them it was because I wasn't bi at all, I'd been stringing him along for years, I had only ever been with women, and being blown by a guy didn't make me gay. It stuck. It stuck so well that the hangout invites trickled to a close, and the friends I shared my coming out with decided I belonged back in the closet.

So now I'm in the bedroom of a very eager man, who doesn't realize my jaw is clenched through our kisses, but I'd like it if I wasn't faking it, so I— "Stop."

For a terrifying moment, he doesn't, and I say it again and again and am about to push him away when he draws back. *Stop*.

CAPITAL PRIDE

OREAD FRIAS

We roam the festival.
Shoulder to shoulder, hand to palm;
I did not know I could love like this.
You gave me rainbow-tinted shades,
and I have found a rainbow-striped
bucket hat to match.
Tangy overpriced lemonade
keeps away the heat.
A bag holds
water, first aid kit,
earrings, stickers, a lovely fan,
a print of plants in person-shape.
I am encompassed in life:
Your fingers take mine, and we find
pop-up bookstores with graphic novels
and sapphic lit. Blind date with a book.
Weed—pre-rolls and edibles—
and shroomery of all sorts.
Trucks with funnel cake
and too many types of meat.
Someone has a dick popsicle.
I point out a lesbian couple
with matching shirts that say

#vagitarian, and we share
in the joy of the pun.
An artist sells tasteful nudes,
and is raking in cash.
Another person with a dick popsicle.
Kings and queens of drag
consort with furries.
There are so many shirtless men,
and the asexuals
have founded a small nation
on the steps of a grey-brick building.
You and I float in this brackish of queers,
grounded only by the weight of our bodies.
When I find the dick popsicle stand
I learn they also sell vagina popsicles,
which they call a lickety split.
All of us sweat in the sun:
black and brown and white
and every other shade;
big and skinny, fit and flabby;
everyone who's overdressed
or in their underwear;
anyone of any ability and class;
tits out; ass out; thick hairy chest out.

We're all so hot. We're all a little tired.
Some of us want to go home. And we do.
You say there is a blister on your ankle,
and ask for a band-aid. I provide.
As we walk, I can only think to myself:
I love you, I love you, I love you.

TRANSEXUALLY CONSTRUCTED LESBIAN-FEMINIST CENTO

TONEE MAE MOLL

Feat. Adrienne Rich & Sharon Olds

Could you imagine a world of women only,
this love between us, this blind love?
Galaxies of women, there
one says *I am a weapon thrown down.* Let there be no more killing
of daughter, sisters, lovers caught in the crossfire.
All the women I grew up with are sitting
underwater, in silence and darkness.
I look at my face in the glass and see
back to a self which had been waiting, for me,
my girlhood frozen in to forms:
buttocks, backs of the knees, the cock.
her wounds came from the same source as her power
I am taking the word *love* away from that
the sea is not a question of power
out here at the end of the world.

Because the cento is a form that exclusively uses lines from other poets and collages them into a new context, this poem is made up of alternating lines from Adrienne Rich and Sharon Olds.

ARS POETICA FOR THE GAY BITCHES WITH TOO MANY TOTE BAGS

ELI V. RAHM

She bought flowers from the back of a blue truck and
gave them to me, the petals a haze of red—orgasmic this
color, kinky and tender and somehow this has become
another sex poem, the movement of the bags like bodies,
how they shape to what's put inside swollen as bellies like
how you press against me, your hips, and yes this is
before I knew you, before the only person to buy me
flowers was my best friend, and like these bags, she is a
collection of much loved things, of items we can't bear to
leave the house without and I mean *thing* in the most
loving of ways like the stuffed animals we keep in our bed
and call our babies—how the inanimate is just as real
as you believe them to be and in this, you joke, we are
just like dragons blowing red air over all we love, all we hold
and keep, close.

IS HOMOSEXUALITY CONTAGIOUS?

NATASHA SAJÉ

Like where you touch a doorknob and then wipe your eye and two days later you have a scratchy throat? *Or a restaurant patron*

seeing Baked Alaska at another table flaunt its frosted heat, tender cake under cold fruity creaminess and fluffy mountains of meringue. You've heard of it.

You're born that way. Either liking women or men or both and in-between. Or neither. Or not knowing or at least not knowing yet. Or wanting to know. Or not.

Watch the person move their spoon into the mound.

The Romans. Look what happened to them.

Mike Pence calls his wife "mother."

Hear a faint smack of lips.

Their daughter wrote a story about a rabbit based on Marlon Brando.

If we're talking about animals, recall the two male penguins who raised an orphan chick. Or the half female-half male cardinal. You could *see* the split.

That's genetic. Abominations, etc. Can we blame

Augustine who thought he could live without a body and wanted everyone else
to do the same.

Yada, yada, yada. Which means "know" in Hebrew. Or to show mercy.

Each of us has things we must turn away from. Look

but don't touch. Think but don't act. Don't think too hard, actually. Feel.

No, don't feel.

The whole room orders the flaming thing.

Because you weren't really hungry.

WATER CYCLE

TANYA OLSON

As a husband I would struggle
I would struggle as a husband
The struggle of the husband
like the struggle of the rain
Always falling Never rising
Unless as steam Unless as changed

How does rain return to clouds
Homework question Kitchen table
Ask your father says the mother
He hunts He farms He comes He goes
It seems like something he should know

Do you remember Remember mother
How she held you How you dangled
Remember father How he knew things
How he left How he came home

How would I know says the father
Home again Not yet leaving
After dinner Meat Starch Coffee
A time for questions *Sounds like science*
So spelling words Test tomorrow

Antique Robber Davenport
Let us know what you find out

Husbands lucky Fathers lucky
First they're here Then they're there
Condensation Evaporation
Liquid Gas Liquid again
Rain 101 Should have learned it
Must have missed that day in school

The water cycle has seven stages
Runoff Storage Evaporation
Condensation Precipitation
Interception Infiltration
Percolation Transpiration

Transpiration is exhalation
How plants lose water
Why plants need rain
I too would dangle if a mother
If a mother children would sway
As a husband I too would struggle
If a husband I would fail to stay

PERMANENT RESIDENT, WITHOUT GREEN CARD

YERMIYAHU AHRON TAUB

You could find yourself a room. Elsewhere. Far from or close to here. In a respectable house. Furnished. Small, well-appointed. A bed. A desk. A small icebox. Madam Sunderlin sees to the comfort of all of her "guests." There would be meals shared or brought to your room. There, you might consider in moonlight our once-bounty. The choreography of our days, our decades that followed the jubilation of our foundational canopy evening, the ambiguity of our nuptial night. The ways in which banality can glow when left unre-cited. What we were. Creations matched long ago, forged in the benediction of the Divine, in the formulas and dia-grams of Kabbalah. And you might consider what you want now. What will be available to you now. For your options will be diminished. Word will have gotten out. Without my having seen to that. The moon's light will generate insight if you remain open to the pallor of its beams, to the deter-mination in their progress. If insight isn't thus generated, don't blame the moon. Or the stars, for that matter. Look within. Or you could spread out your favorite volumes of verse on the spindly yet strangely sturdy writing desk. Per-haps even pen some of your own, again, that is, if you are at ease with the moon. It's all a question of synchronicity so don't blather on about the "block" that has plagued you and your ilk. I won't be there to hear it, in any case. Nor will anyone else. You could stroll the small square several blocks from the house, with its tidy paths, box hedges, spruces, where the stone angel spreads her wings of magnanimity over all who cross her path and even those who don't, where others similarly or dissimilarly situated sometimes linger into the night. You all know how to be seen and not seen in the streetlights' radiance. Since you cannot bring them to your own room, you may even dare to go home with one or more of them in carefully timed intervals or in sudden bursts of hunger and audacity. Remember, the more you engage, the more risk you incur. They may be repelled by the perfume of me, by the stench of your rebuff—no, your abandonment—of me still hovering on your jacket collar. For yes, it was abandonment, although you may call it self-discovery, the discovery, finally, of your true self. Or you may convince them to hold their nose, tantalize them with some sort of reward. The promise of ... well ... whatever little it is that you can promise. You may find fleeting reprieve in their hard, indifferent thrusts, in a room you might otherwise never have found yourself had you not trashed the prescience of the Zohar. Perhaps overlooking the docks. Or the pencil factories. Or the slaughterhouses. No matter. When you leave, when you're back in your room, I will be there, too. I won't go into what I will do. I haven't decided yet. But I will be there, too. The anguish of my nights will ravage your resources for rest. The white knuckles of my rage will silence the siren song of sleep.

HELLO

ERIC HOUSE

On my first Friday night out as a single gay man in a big gay city, I was too scared to go into a queer bar by myself, so I didn't. How pathetic it must be to be 24 and not know what I want to order besides a Bud Light that'll make me gassy. I pass the door and head into a fancy restaurant named Le Diplomate just so I can piss in their nice bathrooms and say yes, I've certainly been there, the bread is marvelous, or whatever. It must be.

I blink to find another ad on a lamp post advertising gay kickball. I can't think of anything more vulnerable than slamming my fat right foot into a rubber ball in front of gorgeous strangers who will undoubtedly kiss and kiss and kiss after the game, and I'll watch, wondering when it would be appropriate to leave to go watch reality television with my parents' cable login. On the way home, the voice of Ben Gibbard sings the lyrics to me again: D.C. sleeps alone tonight.

I text my friend that everything's going great, and I'm so excited for a fresh start. New town, new me, new pills for heartburn. Old habits die long and slowly, oozing down the Brutalist metro enclave and onto my shoulder. I step over mysterious city juice as metro cars blast dense, warm air past my face, and I text my friend again that I don't know where I'm supposed to be standing at any given time. If the past is the end of the train and the future is at the front, I'm somewhere in the middle with shoddy WiFi, trying to re-download another dating app.

After grad school classes I manage not to skip, I swipe left and right and wait. I wait and wait, and the lovers never come, and neither do I. The words of my friend cup them-selves around my ears: Are you even trying? What would it look like if you did?

It might look like this: he sees me, and I see him, and that's it; I get to say the poets were right all along. Or maybe I'm the same as I ever was: selfish, internal, distracted, and too eager for a fight or flight home. I've ignored and been ig-nored before, and the space between was my batting aver-age. The weight of a simple "Hello, how are you?" that goes unanswered rests on top of me where others used to lay, thinking about forever while I thought about how to breathe. Or maybe it was the other way around; I made my-self a blanket on their bodies to warm them up, only for them to throw me off the bed at night when I got too heavy.

One face pops up on the app, and he looks like home, so I type the five-letter word as my heart shoves itself into my ribs. While I wait for his reply, I walk up Connecticut Avenue just to see how far I can get before my blood sugar drops out of me and onto the pavement. I cool myself down in a CVS, spending way too much time debating between SPF 30 and 40 and 50 while "Hold On" by Wilson Phillips blasts down my wet spine. I ditch the debate and spend what little money I have on three consecutive films at a local theater and make myself sick on buckets of day-old popcorn. Someone on the screen is in love and I resist the urge to boo at them, even though I know it's not their fault. They're trying their best.

Like waiting for the sun to implode, he replies. We go back and forth, faster and faster, until suddenly I've blinked, and he's standing in front of me at a cocktail bar, and my past is nowhere to be found, at least not where he can see it. He dances with my friend, and I dance with his until both of our friends have left, and it's just us now, standing at the corner of a busy intersection, waiting to see who steps into it first. I could get hit by a car, or worse, walk myself home. Instead, I close my eyes and put my foot into the glittering blacktop, and hope for the best, whatever that looks like. Maybe when I open my eyes, he'll still be there, hand around mine, all because I said hello first.

CAPITAL QUEER CONTRIBUTORS

Chris Biles (she/her) currently lives and works in Washington, D.C., where she enjoys playing with the light and the dark and losing herself in music, anything outside, and some words here and there. She is published in several literary magazines, journals, and anthologies in print and online. You can find her at marks-in-the-sand.com / Instagram: @marks.in.the.sand / out walking the city streets.

Caroline Bock is the co-president/prose editor at the Washington Writers' Publishing House. She is a longtime ally of the LGBTQ+ community going back to the 1990s when she organized/promoted 'A Moment Without Television' within the cable industry to mark World AIDS Day and raise awareness of the AIDS crisis. She is the author of *Carry Her Home* (winner of the Fiction Award from the Washington Writers' Publishing House), *Before My Eyes*, and *LIE* as well as the forthcoming *The Other Beautiful People*, her first novel for adults (Regal House Publishing, 2026).

Regie Cabico was born in Baltimore, Maryland and divides their time between the DMV and New York serving as a lead teaching artist for the Kennedy Center and executive director of A Gathering of the Tribes. He's the author of *A Rabbit in Search of a Rolex* (Day Eight, 2023).

Alex Carrigan (he/him) is a Pushcart-nominated editor, poet, and critic from Alexandria, VA. He is the author of *Now Let's Get Brunch* (Querencia Press, 2023) and *May All Our Pain Be Champagne* (Alien Buddha Press, 2022).

Sunu P. Chandy (she/her) is the daughter of immigrants, and lives in DC. Sunu's poetry collection, *My Dear Comrades*, features cover art by Ragni Agarwal. Sunu is also a civil rights attorney and currently a Senior Advisor with Democracy Forward, and a board member with Transgender Law Center. Sunu was also featured as a Queer Women of Washington.

Jona Colson (he/him) is a poet, educator, and translator. His poetry collection, *Said Through Glass*, won the Jean Feldman Poetry Prize from the Washington Writers' Publishing House. He is also the translator of *Aguas/Waters* by Miguel Avero and the co-editor of *This Is What America Looks Like: Poetry and Fiction from D.C., Maryland, and Virginia* (2021) and *America's Future* (2025). His poems, translations, and interviews have appeared in *Ploughshares, The Southern Review*, *LitHub,* and elsewhere. He is co-president of Washington Writers' Publishing House and edits the bi-weekly journal, *WWPH Writes*. He is a professor of ESL at Montgomery College and lives in Washington, D.C. jonacolson.com

Suzanne Feldman received her Masters in Creative Writing from Johns Hopkins University. She is the author of five novels, including *Absalom's Daughters* (Holt, 2016, starred review in Kirkus) She was a Walter Dakin Fellow at the Sewanee Writers Conference in 2019. Her latest novel, *Sisters of the Great War*, (Mira/HarperCollins, 2021) has been nominated for a Lambda Literary Award. In 2022 she was awarded a grant from the Maryland State Arts Council and won The Washington Writers' Publishing House Fiction Prize for her short story collection, *The Witch Bottle & Other Stories*.

Bree Fram is a colonel and astronautical engineer in the U.S. Space Force. Bree lives in Virginia with her wife and two kids. She is stationed at the Pentagon and is one of the highest-ranking transgender service members in the military. An earlier version of "Frozen" was published on her social media.

Oread Frias, a resident of Virginia, has no idea what she's doing and hopes no one finds out. Her work has appeared in *AmLit Mag, WWPH Writes, The Foundationalist*, and the 2025 DC Pride Poems project. She's working on a collection of video game poetry.

Jose Gutierrez is a local and national long-time human rights and social justice activist, immigration advocate, Latinx LGBTQ historian, artist, writer, and poet. He is the founder of the Jose Gutierrez Archives, the Latino GLBT History Project, the DC Latino Pride, and co-founder of the Rainbow History Project.

Jonathan Harper (he/him) is the author of the story collection *Daydreamers* and the novel *You Don't Belong Here*. He received his MFA from American University and lives in Northern Virginia.

Emily Holland (they/she) is a genderqueer lesbian writer living in Baltimore. Their work appears in publications including *Shenandoah, DIALOGIST*, and *Black Warrior Review*. She is the author of the chapbook *Lineage* (dancing girl press, 2019). They also are the editor of *Poet Lore*, America's oldest poetry journal, and a creative writing instructor.

Eric House (He/Him/His) has lived and worked as a full-time writer and editor in Washington, DC, since 2017. He resides in Eckington with his husband and their 5-year-old tabby Frankie. His short fiction was recently published in a special Pride edition of the Washington Writers Publishing House's bi-weekly literary journal *WWPH Writes*.

Natalie E. Illum (she/her) is a poet, disability activist and singer living in Washington, D.C. She is the recipient of multiple Poetry Fellowship Grants from the D.C. Commission for the Arts and Humanities, a former Jenny McKean Moore Fellow and a Best of the Net and Pushcart Prize Nominee. She was a founding board member of mothertongue, an LGBTQIA open mic that lasted 15 years. Her work has appeared in various publications, and on NPR's Snap Judgement. Natalie has an MFA in Creative Writing from American University. You can find her on Instagram as @poetryrox, and as one half of the band All Her Muses. She loves whiskey, giraffes and plants.

Hiram Larew's latest poetry collection, *This Much Very,* was published by Alien Buddha Press in 2025. HiramLarePoetry.com and PoetryXHunger.com.

Dwayne Lawson-Brown is a father, host, and Crochet Kingpin. Publications include *One Color Kaleidoscope*, *Twenty: 21*, and *Breaking The Blank* (w/ Rebecca Bishophall; Day Eight Books). For More Information: CrochetKingpin.com.

Chanlee Luu is a writer from Southern Virginia. She received her MFA in creative writing from Hollins University and BS in chemical engineering from UVA. She is the winner of the 2024 Jean Feldman Poetry Award from the Washington Writer's Publishing House, which published her debut collection, *The Machine Autocorrects Code to I*. One of her poems was on display at "50 Years of HOPE and HA-HAs," a Vietnamese American art exhibition.

Saundra Rose Maley is the author of *Disappearing Act,* and a noted scholar of the poet James Wright who coedited Wright's *Selected Letters* and two books on Wright and translation.

Dr. Tonee Mae Moll is a queer & trans writer & educator. Her debut memoir, *Out of Step*, won the 2018 Lambda Literary Award, and was featured that year on the American Library Association's annual list of notable LGBTQ+ books. Tonee Mae's poetry has also received the Adele V. Holden award for creative excellence and the Bill Knott Poetry Prize. She is, most notably, a Gemini.

Evan O'Connor is an aspiring author and ICU nurse in Washington, D.C. His work has been previously published in Washington Writers' Publishing House, *Freedom Fiction Journal*, and Black Hare Press.

Tanya Olson lives in Silver Spring, Maryland. She is the author of *Boyishly, Stay,* and *Born Backwards*, all out from Yes-Yes Books. She has received a Discovery/Boston Review prize and an American Book Award and was been named a Lambda Fellow by the Lambda Literary Foundation. Born Backwards was named a top ten 2024 LGBTQ+ work by *Foreword Reviews*.

Michelle Parkerson is from Washington, DC. Her creative career gained impetus in the late 1970s and early 80s, as she became a major contributor to a new Black gay and lesbian renaissance of artists, musicians, activists, writers, and performers in the city—among them, her close friend, poet Essex Hemphill. Since the publication of her first book of poems and short fiction, *Waiting Rooms* (Common Ground Press),

Michelle's poetry and prose have occasionally been anthologized, most recently in *Mouths of Rain* (The New Press).

Eli V. Rahm is a queer writer from Virginia. Their work is featured in *Sugar House Review, Passages North, Bellingham Review, The Cortland Review*, *The Academy of American Poets*, among others. They also have a cat named Bagel.

Kim Roberts is the author of seven books of poems, most recently *Q&A for the End of the World*, a collaboration with poet Michael Gushue (WordTech Editions, 2025). Her second guidebook, *Buried Stories: Walking Tours of Washington, DC-Area Cemeteries*, will be published by Rivanna Books this fall. She lives in DC. kimroberts.org

Natasha Sajé is the author of five books of poems, including, most recently, *The Future Will Call You Something Else* (Tupelo, 2023). Her prose books are a postmodern poetry handbook, *Windows and Doors: A Poet Reads Literary Theory* (Michigan, 2014) and a memoir-in-essays, *Terroir: Love, Out of Place* (Trinity, 2020). Sajé has been teaching in the Vermont College of Fine Arts MFA in Writing Program since 1996. She lives in Washington, DC. "Is Homosexualoity Contagious?" was previously published in *The Future Will Call You Something Else.*

Based near D.C., **Ava Serra** (they/she) is a disabled, non-binary writer exploring light topics such as: disordered menstruation, displaced Boricua culture, abusive survival confessionalism, domestic sapphic joy, and cautionary eco-horror. They are a poetry student at the University of Maryland's MFA program. For more about their work, visit avaserra.com.

Luke Sutherland is a trans writer and librarian living in Washington, D.C. His work has appeared in *smoke and mold*, *ANMLY*, *Bright Wall/Dark Room*, *MQR Mixtape*, and more. He was a finalist for the *SmokeLong Quarterly* Award for Flash Fiction. In his free time, Luke helps organize a trans writing group that aims to build queer literary community in DC. You can find him on Twitter or Instagram @lukejsuth.

Yermiyahu Ahron Taub is a poet and writer in English and Yiddish and a translator of Yiddish literature into English. He is the author of two books of fiction and six volumes of poetry, including *The Education of a Daffodil: Prose Poems/ Di bildung fun a geln nartsis: prozelider* (2017). His translations from the Yiddish include *Dineh: An Autobiographical Novel* by Ida Maze (2022) and *Blessed Hands: Stories* by Frume Halpern (2023). Please visit his website at yataubdotnet.wordpress.com.

Piérre Ramon Thomas is the author of *The Nomadic Poet*. Published works of his can be seen in T*he Mid-Atlantic Review,* *WWPH Writes*, and *BlueInk*. Thomas calls Fairfax home and will be pursuing an MFA in Creative Writing in the fall of 2025. Currently, he's working on a memoir.

Charlotte Van Schaack is an early career writer and editor whose work has been featured in *AmLit Magazine* and *WWPH Writes*. She hails from Greensboro, North Carolina, but has spent the last few years in Washington D.C. attending American University. In 2024, they were an Inner Loop writer-in-residence.

Dan Vera is a Borderlands-born, Queer-Tejano, DC-based writer and editor. Recipient of the Oscar Wilde Award for Poetry and the Letras Latinas/Red Hen Poetry Prize, he's the co-editor of *Imaniman: Poets Writing In The Anzaldúan Borderlands* (Aunt Lute) and author of two books of poetry, *Speaking Wiri Wiri* (Red Hen) and *The Space Between Our Danger and Delight* (Beothuk Books).

Bernard Welt's poetry and essays have appeared in many journals, art catalogs, and anthologies, including *The Best American Poetry*. MA Writing, The Johns Hopkins University; PhD Literary Studies, The American University. National Endowment for the Arts Creative Writers Fellowship and Lambda Literary Awards nomination.

Washington Writers' Publishing House is a non-profit, cooperative literary press that has published over 100 volumes of poetry, fiction, creative nonfiction, and works in translation since 1975. The press sponsors three annual competitions for writers living in DC, Maryland, and Virginia, and the winners of each category comprise the annual slate. In 2021, WWPH launched an online literary journal, *WWPH Writes,* to expand our mission to further the creative work of writers in our region. In 2024, WWPH launched our biennial works in translation series and the WWPH Literary Salons, bringing writers and the literary arts into communities. More about the Washington Writers' Publishing House at www.washingtonwriters.org.

We are thankful for the support of the **DC Commission on the Arts & Humanities** for helping make *Capital Queer: A Pride Celebration from Washington Writers' Publishing House* possible.

www.ingramcontent.com/pod-product-compliance
Lightning Source LLC
Chambersburg PA
CBHW021933170626
46807CB00007B/3082